ISBN# 978-164945328-0

Published by: June Pinkham Publishing
Rollinsford, New Hampshire
junepinkham@msn.com

Illustrated by: Aaron Risi

HONEY CARES

BY JUNE WHITTIER PINKHAM

Follow the adventures of best friends Lee, the Lion, Evee, the Bunny, and Honey the Badger as they embark on the first of their many musical adventures around the world!

Based on a true story.

For Leora (Lee) and Everett (Evee)

Honey was fearless.
Everyone said so.
She climbed the highest mountains,
And swam the seas below.

Honey was a badger.
And badgers, they say,
Don't care, not at all.
Nothing gets in their way.

Honey was brave.
She never gave in.
If there was a battle,
She always would win.

Her best
friends
were
Evee and Lee,
And anyone could see,
Those three were as fearless
and brave as could be.

One day they hiked,
On a daring new road.
It was rocky and rough,
But they were brave and bold.

Suddenly they saw,
A very strange thing!
It was made of wood,
And it had four strings!

And blurry words on it.
"What is it?" asked Lee.
Honey squinted to read,
"It says 'uku...lay' Lee."

Lee asked, "It says what?"
"It says 'uku...lay' Lee."

"Oh, I see," said Evee. "A ukulele."

Honey shrugged and wondered,
What does it do?
As she plucked at a string,
A beautiful sound came through!

Honey roared! Lee jumped!
What magic is this?
A sound so happy,
That no one could miss!

In fact, from the fields,
And the streams and the trees,
Came hundreds of creatures,
With faces of glee!

There came squirrels and bears,
And foxes so fair,
Giraffes, and elephants,
Even tigers from their lair.

"We heard the sound
Of your happy uku-lay.
And we wanted to sing
And to dance and to play!"

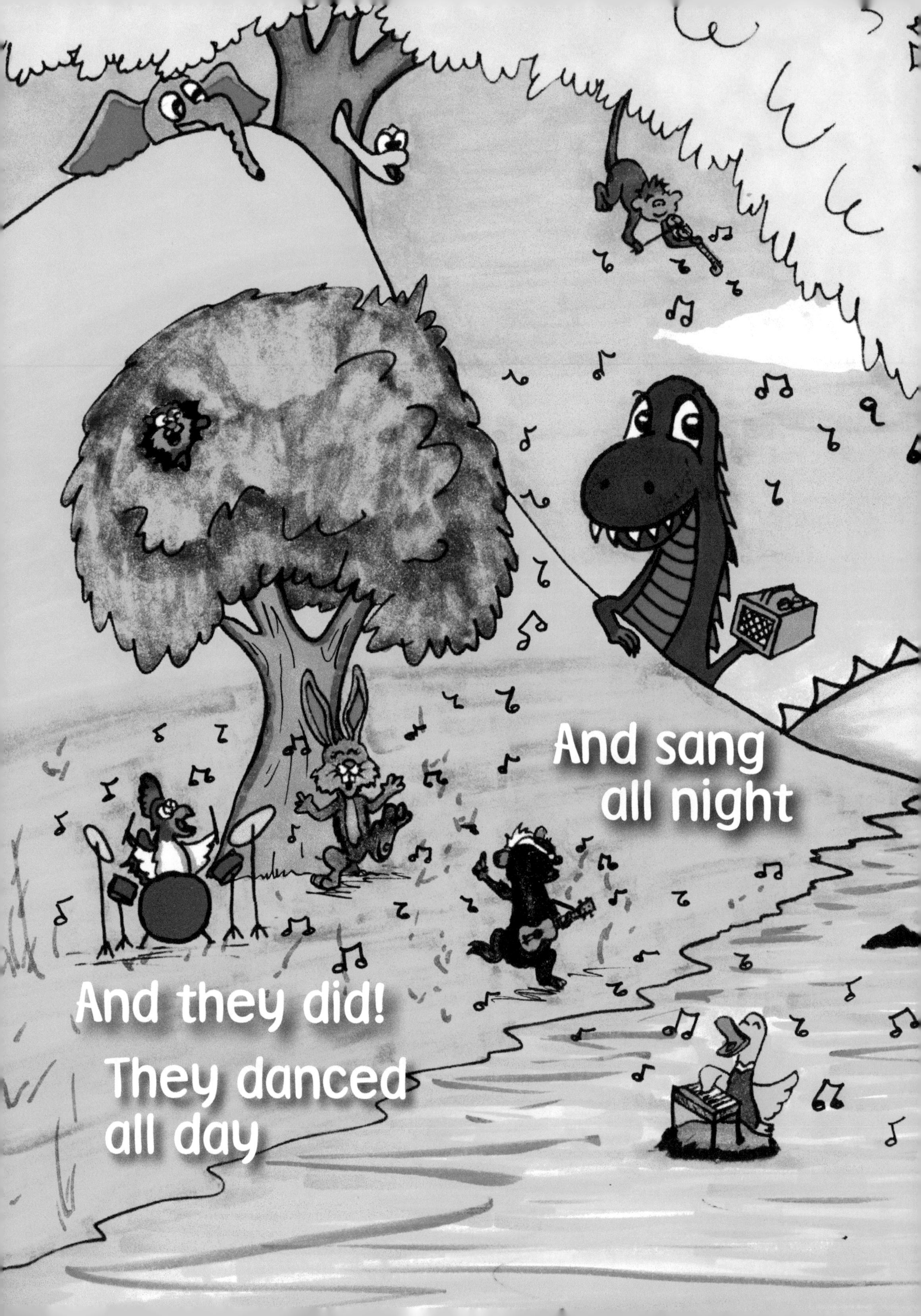

And they did!

They danced all day

And sang all night

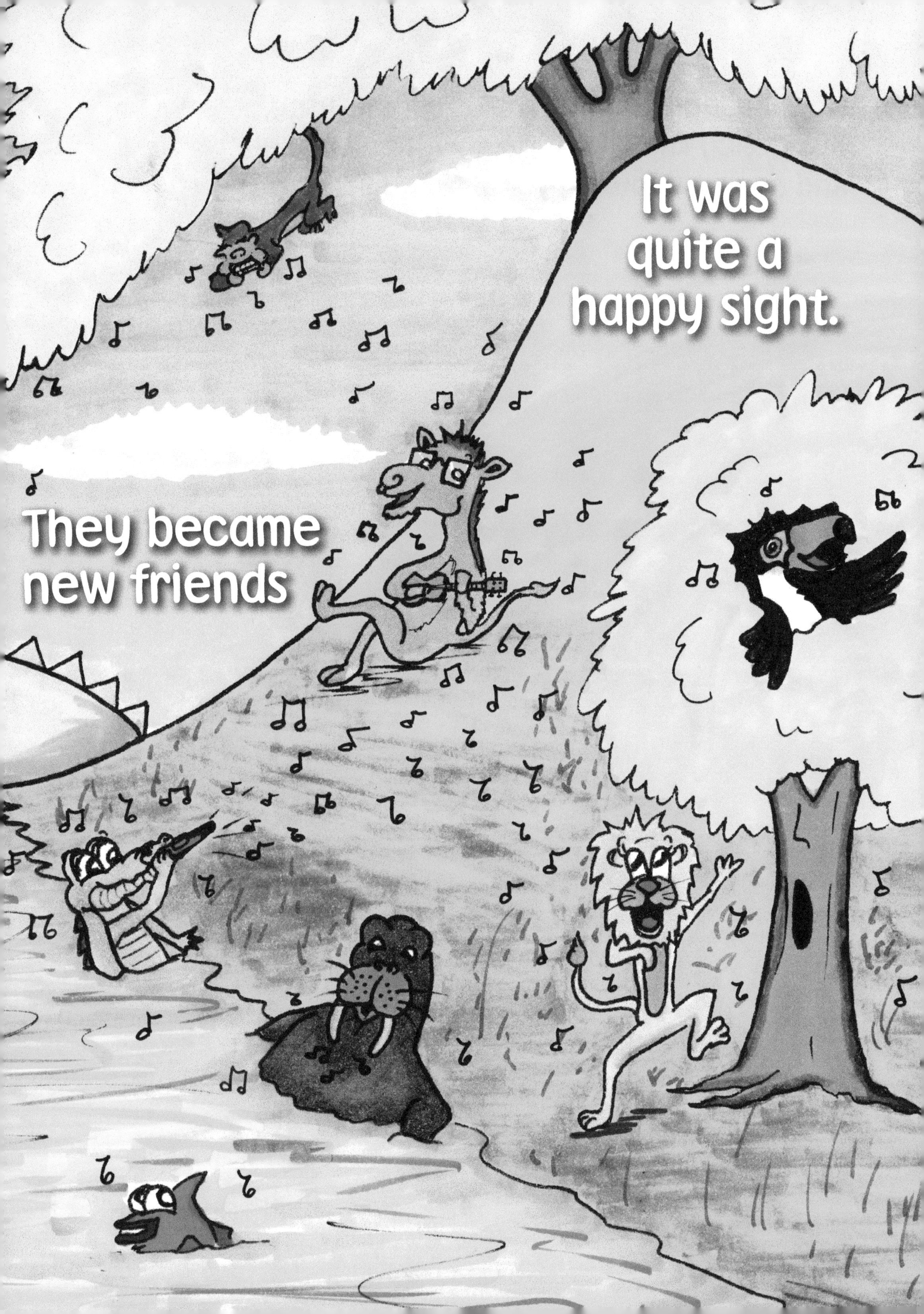
They became new friends
It was quite a happy sight.

Now, Badgers, don't care at all, they say,
But Honey knew, that day, with her ukulele,
And her new-found friends, and music to share,

That, the truth, after all is,
Badgers DO care.

THE END

June Pinkham, from Rollinsford, New Hampshire is an accomplished accountant who has never misplaced a decimal point. She also holds the title of the World's Most Okayest UBass Player and uses that title for the good of all mankind (and as a member of the feisty band "June and the Honey Badgers"). June supports the Ukulele Kids Club, a charity that brings smiles (and ukuleles!) to hospitalized children.

She hopes those who enjoy this book may consider a contribution to the UKC by visiting https://theukc.org/

Illustrator/author/composer Aaron Risi has worked professionally for 20 years.
See more at AaronRisi.com.